Snow

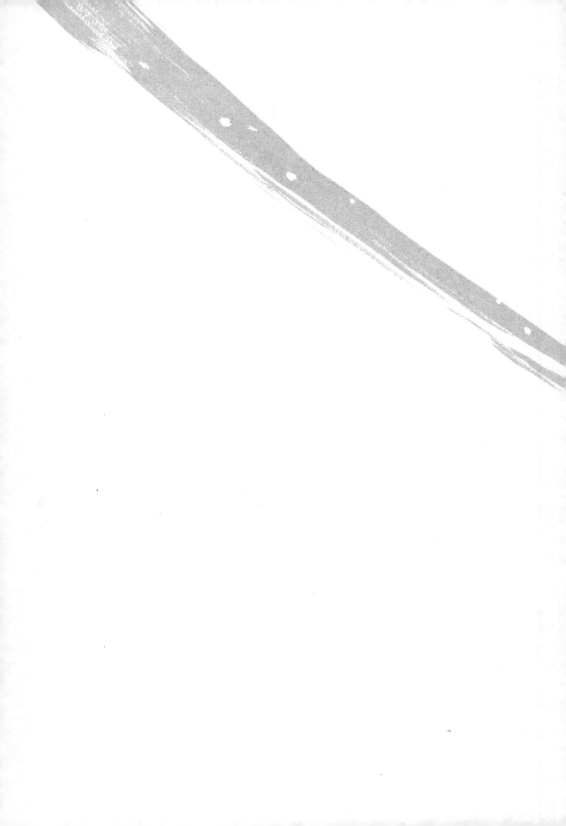

Snow

Roy McKié and P. D. Eastman

BEGINNER BOOKS
A DIVISION OF RANDOM HOUSE, INC.

This title was originally cataloged by the Library of Congress as follows: McKie, Roy. Snow [by] Roy McKie and P.D. Eastman. [New York] Beginner Books [1962] 61 p. illus. 24 cm. (Beginner books, B-27) I. Eastman, Philip D., joint author. II. Title. PZ8.3.M223Sn   62–15114 ISBN 0-394-80027-3   ISBN 0-394-90027-8 (lib. bdg.)

Snow!

Snow! Snow!

Come out in the snow.

4

Snow! Snow!
Just look at the snow!
Come out! Come out!
Come out in the snow.

I want to know
If you like snow.
Do you like it?
Yes or no?

Oh yes! Oh yes!
I do like snow.

Do you like it
In your face?

Yes!

I like it any place.

What is snow?
We do not know.
But snow is lots of fun,
We know.

What makes it snow?
We do not know.

But snow is fun
To dig and throw.

Snow is good
For me and you,
For men and women,
Horses, too.

Snow is good.

It makes you slide.

It lets you give

Your dog a ride.

Snow is good
For making tracks . . .

And making pictures
With your backs.

We go up hill.

The snow is deep.

We can't go fast.

The hill is steep.

We think our dog

Has gone to sleep.

But then we get
Up top at last.
Then down we come.
We come down fast!

Sometimes we put on

Long, long feet

And walk up

Every hill we meet.

Down hill we fly!
Down hill we sail!
Our dog sails after,
On his tail.

28

What a silly
Thing to do!
Are your feet
Too long for you?

Come on! Get up!

Get on your way!

We have a lot

To do today.

Now take some snow
And make a ball.

A lot of snow balls
Make a wall.

Put on more snow balls
One by one.
Our house of snow
Will soon be done.

Do you like bread?

Do you like meat?

Come in our house.

Come in and eat.

Snow is lots of fun,
All right!
It gives you
A big appetite.

We had our bread.

We had our meat.

Some bread is left

For birds to eat.

43

Now make another

Ball of snow.

Push it! Push it!

See it go.

What a snow ball!

See it grow!

See it grow

And grow and grow!

What will we make?

Let's make a man!

Let's make the biggest

Man we can!

We will call

Our snow man Ned.

But first

He has to have a head.

His head will have
To have a hat.
His hat is on.
Just look at that!
He is so big.
He is so tall.
He is the biggest
Man of all!

51

The sun! That sun!
It came out fast.
Do you think Ned
Is going to last?

Keep that sun
Away from Ned!
That sun is going
To his head.

The biggest snow man

Of them all

Is very, very,

Very small.

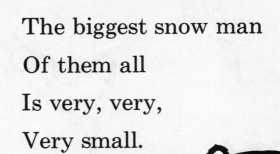

The way that sun
Is coming down,
There soon will be
No snow in town!
Take some! Save it
From the sun!
Take all you can
And run! Run! Run!

The snow out there
Will come and go,
But snow will keep
In here, we know.

So we will put
This snow away
And play with it
Some other day.

61